# MONKEY WALK

COLLEEN MADDEN

**Clarion Books**

Houghton Mifflin Harcourt

Boston    New York

Clarion Books
3 Park Avenue
New York, New York 10016

Clarion Books is an imprint of
Houghton Mifflin Harcourt Publishing Company.

hmhco.com

Library of Congress Cataloging-in-Publication Data
Names: Madden, Colleen M., author, illustrator.
Title: Monkey Walk / Colleen Madden.
Description: Boston ; New York : Clarion Books, Houghton Mifflin Harcourt,
[2018] | Summary: "At the zoo with her family, a girl mopes around until
she is asked to help rescue the zoo's penguins from boredom"— Provided by publisher.
Identifiers: LCCN 2017008210 | ISBN 9780544888982 (hardcover)
Subjects: | CYAC: Zoos—Fiction. | Monkeys—Fiction. | Penguins—Fiction. | Boredom—
Fiction.
Classification: LCC PZ7.1.M259 Mon 2018 | DDC [E]—dc23
LC record available at https://lccn.loc.gov/2017008210

Manufactured in China
SCP 10 9 8 7 6 5 4 3 2 1
4500696719

We traded. Give it back.

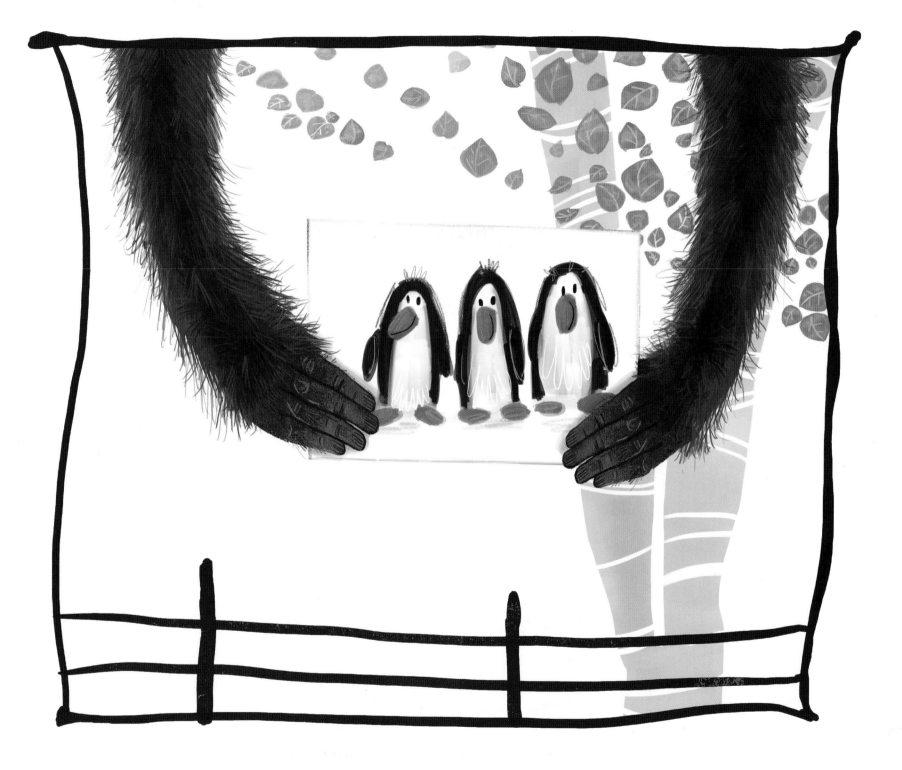

oh,
You have **got**
to be kidding.